RAINBOW MIST SCHOOL
CLASS GOLDEN FEATHER

My name is: .....Comet..........

My best friend is: .....My twin sister, Destiny...

My favourite colour is: .....Purple...........

My favourite food is: .....Hay............

.....I like to look after.....

.....my sister..........

RAINBOW MIST SCHOOL
CLASS GOLDEN FEATHER

My name is: .....Destiny............

My best friend is: .....My twin brother, Comet....

My favourite colour is: All the colours of the rainbow

My favourite food is: .....Grass............

.....I like to do dares and.....

.....get into mischief!..........

Sue Bentley's books for children often include animals, fairies and wildlife. She lives in Northampton and enjoys reading, going to the cinema and watching the birds on the feeders outside her window. She loves horses, which she thinks are all completely magical. One of her favourite books is *Black Beauty*, which she must have read at least ten times. At school she was always getting told off for daydreaming, but she now knows that she was storing up ideas for when she became a writer. Sue has met and owned many animals, but the wild creatures in her life hold a special place in her heart.

Sue Bentley

Magic Ponies

Showjumping Dreams

Illustrated by Angela Swan

PUFFIN

To Beauty – who helped me gain confidence

PUFFIN BOOKS

Published by the Penguin Group
Penguin Books Ltd, 80 Strand, London WC2R 0RL, England
Penguin Group (USA) Inc., 375 Hudson Street, New York, New York 10014, USA
Penguin Group (Canada), 90 Eglinton Avenue East, Suite 700, Toronto, Ontario, Canada M4P 2Y3
(a division of Pearson Penguin Canada Inc.)
Penguin Ireland, 25 St Stephen's Green, Dublin 2, Ireland (a division of Penguin Books Ltd)
Penguin Group (Australia), 250 Camberwell Road, Camberwell, Victoria 3124, Australia
(a division of Pearson Australia Group Pty Ltd)
Penguin Books India Pvt Ltd, 11 Community Centre, Panchsheel Park, New Delhi – 110 017, India
Penguin Group (NZ), 67 Apollo Drive, Rosedale, North Shore 0632, New Zealand
(a division of Pearson New Zealand Ltd)
Penguin Books (South Africa) (Pty) Ltd, 24 Sturdee Avenue, Rosebank,
Johannesburg 2196, South Africa

Penguin Books Ltd, Registered Offices: 80 Strand, London WC2R 0RL, England

puffinbooks.com

First published 2009
3

Text copyright © Sue Bentley, 2009
Illustrations copyright © Angela Swan, 2009
All rights reserved

The moral right of the author and illustrator has been asserted

Set in Bembo
Made and printed in England by Clays Ltd, St Ives plc

British Library Cataloguing in Publication Data
A CIP catalogue record for this book is available from the British Library

ISBN: 978–0–141–32596–5

www.greenpenguin.co.uk

Prologue

Comet folded his magnificent golden
wings as his shining hooves touched
down on the grassy plain. The magic
pony gave a whinny of excitement.
It felt good to be home on Rainbow
Mist Island.

But his happiness lasted only a moment
as he thought of his twin sister. Destiny
had been lost for so long. Surely she must

have returned safely by now.

The scent of the sweet grass reminded
Comet that he was very hungry so he
lowered his head and began eating.
Sunbeams slanted through the swirling
multicoloured mist that gave the island its
name. They gleamed on his cream coat
and gold mane and tail.

Chewing, Comet looked up, scanning
the landscape for signs of any of the other
horses that belonged to the Lightning
Herd. His large deep violet eyes widened
as he caught a movement.

There, behind those scrubby trees!

Comet could see a long shadow
stretching across the grass. His pale coat
twitched with nerves as he stiffened.
Was it another magic pony or one of the
fierce dark horses, who wanted to steal

the Lightning Herd's magic?

Comet hesitated, weighing up the danger. 'Destiny?'

The magic pony's lonely heart quickened with longing as he thought of his twin sister who he missed so much. He snorted, deciding to take a risk, and cantered towards the trees.

Just as Comet reached them, the low branches parted and an older horse with a wise expression and calm gold eyes stepped out.

'Blaze!' Swallowing his disappointment, Comet bowed his head before the leader of the Lightning Herd.

'I am glad to see you again, my young friend,' Blaze said in a deep neigh. 'But I am afraid that Destiny has not returned to us.'

Comet sighed deeply. 'She must still think she is in terrible trouble for losing the stone.'

The stone of Power protected the Lightning Herd from the dark horses. Destiny had accidentally lost it when she and Comet were cloud-racing. Comet had recovered the stone, but Destiny had already fled.

Blaze nodded gravely. 'I do not think she will come back, unless you find her and explain all is now well.'

Comet's beautiful violet eyes flashed with purpose. 'I will go to the other world and search for her!'

'We must ask the stone's help to find where she is hiding.' Blaze stamped his foot and pawed at the grass. A fiery opal appeared, which swirled with flashes of multicoloured light.

The magic pony looked down and peered deeply into the rainbow depths. The stone grew larger and rays of dazzling light spread outwards.

An image formed in the glowing centre. Comet gasped as he saw Destiny standing beneath a spreading tree in a world far away.

'I will leave at once!' he whinnied.

There was a bright flash of dazzling violet light, and rainbow mist surrounded Comet. The pale cream pony, with his flowing golden mane and tail, and gleaming gold-feathered wings, disappeared. In his place stood a handsome palomino pony with a warm caramel-coloured coat, a sandy mane and tail and glowing deep violet eyes.

'Use this disguise. Find your twin sister and return with her safely,' Blaze urged.

'I will!' Comet vowed.

The magic pony's caramel coat bloomed with violet sparks. Comet snorted as he felt the power building inside him. And the shimmering rainbow mist whooshed into a whirlpool as it drew Comet in . . .

Chapter
ONE

'Go on, Alex! Go for it!' Zoe cried.

With her best friend shouting encouragement, Alexandra Judd gritted her teeth and concentrated hard as she rode towards the final fence. If Pasha soared over this one too, it would be a clear round.

Her mum and dad were in the crowd watching the horse trials event. She

hoped she could make them proud. It
would be great to win a rosette to take
home.

Alex sat tall, looked straight ahead
and kept her heels down. Strands of her
shoulder-length brown hair blew out
from under her riding hat.

'One! Two! Th–' she said under her
breath. 'Oh!' At the last moment, her
chestnut pony seemed to miss a step.

Pasha swung her hind legs sideways,

just avoiding banging into the fence. But
with a whinny of pain, the pony sank on
to her haunches. Alex only just managed
to stay on as Pasha scrambled to her feet
and stood with her head hanging down.

Alex gasped with dismay as she realized
that something was badly wrong.

Dismounting quickly and trying to
fight down panic, she led her pony away
from the course. 'Poor girl. Have you
hurt yourself?' she said gently. 'Come on,
slowly now. Let's get the vet to look at
you. She'll make you better.'

As she led the limping pony to one
side, her mum and dad were already
racing towards her. Alex gave up all
pretence of being calm.

'Mum! Dad! Something's happened to
Pasha!' she wailed.

9

'All right, love. You're doing all the
right things.' Her dad took over. He
bent and swiftly ran his hand down the
injured pony's back leg. Pasha flinched
and tremors ran over her chestnut coat.
'I hope it's just a sprain and not a torn
ligament.'

A torn ligament was serious. A feeling
of dread jolted through Alex as she saw
her parents exchanging serious looks.
She'd had Pasha for three years and loved
her to bits. She couldn't bear to think of
the plucky little chestnut pony being in
pain.

A voice came over the loudspeaker.
'Vet to showjumping, please. Right away.'

It seemed like hours before the van
arrived and the vet was examining Pasha
with her expert eye. Alex stood with her

arms round her pony's warm neck, trying hard not to cry. 'Don't be scared, Pasha. The vet's a kind lady. She's going to help you,' she said gently.

Mrs Judd put a hand on her daughter's arm. 'Why don't you go and wait with Zoe, love? She looks worried to death for you over there. We'll take care of Pasha. I'll call you over the moment the vet's finished.'

Alex didn't want to leave Pasha, but she nodded miserably. She walked over to her best friend who was standing a few metres away with Maxi, her brown-and-white Welsh pony.

Zoe looked close to tears too. 'Poor Pasha. What an awful thing to happen. Is she going to be OK?' she asked.

'I don't know. The vet's still examining

her,' Alex gulped, grateful that Zoe was
there. They lived a few kilometres away
from each other up at Denton Moor and
had known each other since they were
tiny. Both pony mad, they did everything
together.

Alex swallowed, blinking away unshed
tears. A horrible thought was preying on
her mind. 'Was . . . was it my fault? I'm
not as good at jumping as you are. I . . .
I might have done something wrong and
it made Pasha land awkwardly.'

Zoe shook her head. 'I don't think so. Everything looked fine from where I was.'

Alex nodded slowly, hoping that Zoe was right and not just saying that to make her feel better.

The wait was almost unbearable, but eventually the vet was finished. The moment the vet dusted off her hands and rose to her feet, Alex rushed back.

'What's wrong with Pasha? Her leg's not broken, is it? She's not going to have to be . . .' She couldn't say the awful words.

'No,' the vet said quickly, banishing her worst fears. 'But it's a bad sprain and she's split her heel. Your pony's going to be out of action for a while she rests that leg.'

Alex was so relieved that Pasha wasn't more seriously hurt that it took a few seconds for the news to sink in. 'But . . .

she is going to get well again?'

The vet nodded. 'There's no reason why she shouldn't make a full recovery. I've given her some medicine, so she'll be more comfortable on the journey home.'

Alex felt faint with relief. She turned and gave Zoe a thumbs-up. Zoe waved back, beaming.

With the vet and her dad helping, they managed to get Pasha safely up the ramp and into their transporter. The big truck-sized horse lorry hadn't been new when they got it recently and there was a dent on one side. Inside, it had room for four ponies and loads of space for equipment.

Once Pasha was tethered in her stall, Alex gave her a handful of oats. 'You were so brave,' she crooned, patting her. 'You have a good rest now.'

Back outside, she felt at a loose end.
Zoe was grooming Maxi and her mum
was making lunch. Her dad suggested
they have a mooch around the show's
stalls, which sold everything from riding
boots to the latest saddle soap.

Alex didn't really fancy it. Pasha's injury had cast a shadow over the day for her. 'Thanks, but do you mind if I go for a walk by myself instead?' she asked him.

'Course not, love. It'll do you good. Don't be too long.'

'I won't.'

She wandered across the lorry park. Riders on ponies and horses passed her on their way to and from the showjumping and dressage enclosures. It was a warm spring day; families were enjoying picnics on the grass as they watched the cross-country.

Alex went through a gateway that led into a small copse. Flame-shaped yellow crocus flowers glowed against the dark soil next to shy purple violets. One or two people were walking their dogs, but

the place was mostly empty. The rich
smells of bark and grass surrounded her.

Alex paused on the shore of a small
lake. She noticed a patch of mist hovering
above the water. It seemed to be drifting
towards her.

Suddenly there was a bright flash
of violet sparkles and a shimmering

cloud filled the entire clearing. Alex saw rainbow droplets glistening on her skin.

'Oh!' She narrowed her eyes, trying to peer through the strange multicoloured mist.

As it began to fade, Alex saw that a pony was walking towards her. It was a palomino with a glossy caramel-coloured coat, a sandy mane and tail, and bright deep violet eyes.

'Can you help me, please?' it asked in a velvety neigh.

Chapter
TWO

Alex froze. She stared at the pretty pony in complete astonishment. She must still be feeling so upset about poor Pasha that she was imagining things! Whoever heard of a pony that could talk?

'What are you doing in here? I wonder who you belong to,' she murmured to herself.

The pony lifted its head proudly and

flared its nostrils. 'I belong to no one.
I am Comet of the Lightning Herd. I
have just arrived here from far away.'

Alex's jaw dropped. 'Y-you *can* talk?
But-but how come?'

'All the other magical Lightning
Horses in my herd can talk,' Comet told
her. 'What is your name?'

Alex swallowed, still not quite believing
that this was happening. She felt like she'd
stumbled into a real live fairy tale.

'I–I'm . . . um, Alexandra Judd, but everyone calls me Alex,' she found herself stammering. 'I'm . . . here at the horse trials with my parents and my best friend, Zoe . . .'

Comet dipped his head in a formal bow and his pale sandy mane swung forward. 'I am honoured to meet you, Alex.'

'Um . . . me too,' Alex said, feeling as if she ought to curtsy or something. 'Did you say that you came from far away? Like a different country?'

'Much further. I live in another world on Rainbow Mist Island with my twin sister, Destiny.'

'Really? Wow! Is she here too? Where is she?' Alex asked, fascinated, looking around for another talking palomino.

Comet shook his head. 'Destiny is here in your world, but she is in hiding. She fled here after the Stone of Power was lost during our game of cloud-racing. This stone protects our herd from the dark horses who want to steal our magic. It has been found, but Destiny does not know this. I have come to find her and take her home.'

Alex blinked at the handsome pony. What he had told her was so magical and strange. She wasn't sure that she could take it all in. But one thing in particular was puzzling her.

'Cloud-racing? What's —' she began.

Comet's violet eyes widened. 'Stay back, please,' he snorted.

Alex felt a strange warm tingling sensation flowing down to her fingertips

as violet sparks ignited in Comet's
caramel-coloured coat and more
shimmering rainbow mist swirled around
him. The palomino had gone and in
its place was a pale cream pony with a
flowing gold mane and tail that sparkled
like spun silk. But it was the wide-spread
gold-feathered wings that sprang from his
shoulders that stole Alex's breath.

'Oh!' She gasped in utter wonder at the magnificent sight. Nothing could have prepared her for anything so beautiful. 'Comet?'

'Yes. It is still me, Alex. Do not be alarmed,' Comet said in a deep velvety whinny.

Before Alex had time to get used to seeing Comet in his true form, there was another spurt of violet sparkles and the multicoloured mist broke into shining dust and disappeared, revealing the palomino pony once more.

'That's an amazing disguise! Can Destiny make herself look like a normal pony too?'

Comet nodded, his ears swivelling. 'But her disguise will not protect her if the dark horses find her. I must search for my sister. Will you help me?'

'Of course I will,' Alex said, even
though she hadn't a clue about where
to start looking. 'Do you think Destiny
might be here at the horse trials?'

Comet twitched his sandy tail. 'I
cannot sense that she is near. We will need
to look for her on the slopes and hills
nearby.'

'It's pretty wild up on the high moors.
There are loads of places among the rocks
and caves where Destiny could hide,' Alex
said thoughtfully. 'I'll be going home to
Scarp Hill Farm in a few hours. I could
ask Mum and Dad if you could come
with me. We're used to looking after
animals. There's loads of room in our
horse lorry, even with two ponies in it
already. That's Pasha, my pony. She's just

gone lame,' she said, feeling a ripple of anxiety. She dragged her attention back to the magic pony. 'And . . . and Maxi, who belongs to Zoe, my best friend. I can't wait to see everyone's faces when I tell them about you!'

'No! You cannot tell anyone my secret,' Comet neighed, his violet eyes serious. 'You must promise me, Alex.'

Alex pressed her lips together. She felt disappointed that she couldn't tell her parents about the amazing pony. But it seemed even worse to keep secrets from Zoe. They usually told each other everything.

She nodded slowly. 'Well – OK then,' she said, prepared to agree if it would keep Comet and Destiny safe from their enemies.

Comet reached out to bump his nose
gently against her arm. 'Thank you.'

'No problem!' Alex smiled and reached
up to stroke him. She rubbed between his
eyes, feeling proud that he had chosen her
for his friend.

'I will come to your home. It will be a
safe place to stay,' Comet neighed.

'Cool! I'd *really* love that. But how am
I going to explain about you and where
you suddenly came from . . .'

'There you are!' called a voice.

Alex spun round to see Zoe running up to her. 'Your mum sent me to find you. Lunch's ready . . . Wow! Who does that gorgeous pony belong to?'

'What pony?' Alex asked, too flustered to think straight.

'Du-uh! The palomino standing right there in front of you!' Zoe pointed at Comet.

'Oh, *that* pony. Well . . . he's . . . um . . .' Alex fumbled for an explanation, before an idea suddenly came to her. 'I . . . er, found him running loose. He probably belongs to someone at the horse trial.'

Alex knew that if she reported Comet no one would be missing this magic pony! They'd probably assume that his owner had left without him and her mum

and dad definitely wouldn't mind looking
after Comet while they waited for him to
be claimed.

Comet nuzzled Alex's shoulder in
gratitude for not giving away his special
secret. 'Thank you, Alex.'

Alex gasped. Comet had just spoken
– in front of Zoe! What could he be
thinking of?

But her friend appeared not to have
noticed anything odd. It was very strange.

Trying to gather her wits, Alex carried
on. She told Zoe that she had found him
loose in the woods. 'I managed to catch
him and calm him down. The owner's
probably going bananas looking for
him,' she said, hoping that she sounded
convincing.

'How awful to lose your pony!' Zoe

29

exclaimed. 'I'd be going mad if Maxi got loose and ran off. Comet? That's a cool name. How do you know that's what he's called?'

'I don't,' Alex said. 'I . . . just thought I'd call him that. He looks like a comet, with his pale mane and tail.'

'It's a lovely name. It really suits him,' Zoe said. 'I'll come with you and help to

find his owner. Hang on, I'll dash back and get a halter and lead rope.'

As Zoe hared off to the transporter, Alex looked at Comet. 'I nearly had kittens when you spoke up in front of her! How come she didn't seem to hear you?'

Comet's eyes gleamed. 'I used my magic so that only you will be able to hear. To anyone else I will seem like an ordinary pony.'

Alex grinned at her special new friend. Comet was anything but ordinary!

Chapter
THREE

As the transporter trundled up the steep road that led to the moors, Alex glanced into the back happily. Three sets of pricked ponies' ears were visible: Pasha's, Maxi's — and Comet's.

Alex hadn't even needed to beg her mum and dad to let Comet come home with them. One look at the handsome palomino and Mrs Judd had fallen in love with him – just as Alex had done – and practically insisted they look after Comet until his owner turned up.

Despite her injury Pasha stood quietly munching hay in the partition next to Comet. It was as if the magic pony's presence had a calming influence on the chestnut pony.

Mr Judd drew to a halt in front of Zoe's house, a rambling stone cottage called Grey Lag House.

Zoe's dad came out and greeted them cheerily. He helped Alex's dad let down the ramp and lead Maxi into the yard. Zoe carried her brown-and-white gelding's tack to the stable.

'Thanks very much for taking us with you,' she called to Alex's parents. She turned to Alex. 'I'll ride over tomorrow morning for some jumping practice. Oh, I forgot – there's no point now is there, with poor Pasha being lame?'

'I guess not.' Alex's spirits sank as she thought how boring the half-term holiday would be, without riding with her best friend. She brightened as a thought came to her. 'Hang on! I'll need to exercise Comet so I may as well ride him while Pasha's getting better.'

Comet nickered agreement from inside the transporter.

'That sounds like the perfect arrangement,' Alex's mum said. 'Finding Comet running loose like that seems to have turned out to be a stroke of luck.'

'Definitely! I'm going to take the *best* care of him!' Alex said with a wide grin. 'I'll see you tomorrow then!' She waved to her friend as they drew away down the track and headed home to Scarp Hill Farm.

Alex couldn't help the eagerness that made her pulse race at the thought of riding the magic pony. She hoped Pasha wouldn't be jealous.

Early the following morning, Alex went to check that her chestnut pony was comfortable. 'Hello there, brave girl,' she crooned, sliding open the door to Pasha's stall. When she'd settled her in last night, she'd been careful to pile clean straw up extra high round the walls to make a deep and comfortable bed.

Pasha was lying down. She lifted her head and looked at Alex with mild eyes. Alex sat down and gently rubbed her soft

brown nose. 'That's right. You just relax
and let that bad old leg get better. The
vet's coming to check on you again later.'

From the next stall, Comet gave a
soft whicker of encouragement. Pasha
nickered back softly and then lay back
down with a contented sigh. Alex gave
her a final pat and made sure she had
food and water, before feeding Comet
and making a start on her usual stable
chores.

She suddenly felt a strange warm
tingling sensation in her fingertips as
bright violet sparks ignited in Comet's
caramel coat. His ears crackled with tiny
rainbow bolts of magical power. Her eyes
widened. What was going on?

She watched in total amazement
as there was a whooshing noise and
thousands of tiny fireflies shot into the air.
Swoosh! Rustle! Shine! They rushed about
swiftly scooping up soiled straw, dropping
it into a wheelbarrow, and busily cleaning
and polishing the bridles hanging on a
nearby hook.

Alex stood by, her hands at her sides,
feeling a bit uncomfortable as there was
nothing for her to do. Soon all the work
was done. The glittery helpers dissolved
into sparkly dust and disappeared. Alex

took a deep breath as she realized there
was something she had to get straight.

'Thanks ever so much for helping me,
Comet. But I really don't mind doing this
work,' she said tactfully. 'Actually, I enjoy
it. It's all part of looking after a pony.'

'I did not think of that. Thank you for
explaining. I will ask if you need help
next time,' Comet neighed.

Alex smiled, glad that her magical friend understood and that she hadn't hurt his feelings. 'Zoe will be here soon. Dad said we could practise jumping in the field. It's going to be fun. Maxi's pretty good. But I've got a feeling that you're going to be even better.'

Comet snorted happily as she led him out of the stable into the yard. 'I like Zoe and Maxi.'

Alex had just finished tacking him up and was tightening the girth round his tummy when she heard hoof-beats. She whirled round with an eager smile, and saw two riders coming up the winding lane towards the farm.

She frowned. 'That's strange. Who's that with Zoe? Oh, it's her cousin, Saffron,' she said, her spirits sinking.

Comet's ears twitched. 'You do not sound pleased.'

'It's just that I was looking forward to having fun today with you, Zoe and Maxi,' Alex admitted. 'It won't be the same with Saffron. Oh well, she's here now. I guess it will be OK. It won't be for that long.'

Comet looked up curiously as the two girls trotted through the farm gate.

Zoe stood up in her stirrups and waved. 'Hi, Alex! Guess what? My aunt and uncle and Saffron have come to stay with me for the school holidays. She can practise jumping with us.'

'Oh, OK.' Alex tried not to sound too churlish but still felt a prickle of dismay at the thought of having to share her best friend for two whole weeks. Saffron was

older than both of them. Alex had only
met her once before and so she didn't
know her all that well.

'Hi, Alex.' Zoe's twelve-year-old cousin
sat on a flashy pony. She wore pink-and-
black gloves that matched her stylish
riding hat cover. Her saddle cloth had her
name on it in glittery writing.

'Hi, Saffron.' Alex forced a smile,
making an effort to be friendly. 'Your
pony's really pretty. What's her name?'

'Sparkly Fairy Princess,' Saffron said.

'Er . . . right. Cool.' But despite the fussy name, the grey pony was truly beautiful, with an elegant head and large dark eyes. Her silvery mane flopped prettily over her forehead.

'Zoe told me what happened at the horse trials. It's rotten luck about Pasha.'

'Yeah. It was pretty awful. The vet says she'll be OK, though,' Alex told her.

'That's good. It's horrible when your pony's lame.' Saffron ran her eyes over Comet. 'That palomino you're looking after seems friendly. What's he like to ride?'

'I haven't had a chance to find out yet. He's called Comet, by the way,' Alex told her. 'I'll be riding him for the first time today.'

Saffron nodded. 'It's always exciting to ride a new pony, isn't it?'

'Yes.' Alex thought Saffron seemed very confident, but also quite friendly. Maybe having her around wouldn't be so bad, after all.

'Saffron's going to give us some hot jumping tips. She really knows her stuff. Uncle Tim's won loads of competitions,' Zoe enthused, smiling.

Alex remembered that the older girl's dad was Tim Hall–Chapman, a top showjumper.

'Yeah! Trust me, by the time I've finished putting you two through your paces, you'll be jumping like professionals,' Saffron said with a determined glint in her eye.

'Um . . . good.' Alex's smile wavered a

bit. She wasn't sure whether Zoe's cousin meant that as a promise or a threat.

Chapter
FOUR

'No, not like that! Do it like *this*!' Saffron instructed bossily, waving her arms as Alex assembled the last jump. 'Hurry up!'

Alex sighed. It had taken the three girls over an hour to set out the course of jumps in the field. And Saffron had found fault with every one of them.

Alex bit back a rude comment as she repositioned the poles for the third time.

Finally, the last fence was in place and Saffron gave her a thumbs-up sign.

'I'm surprised she didn't want me to fetch a ruler to measure the jumps too,' she complained to Comet in a whisper. 'Anyone would think this was a proper showjumping arena!'

Comet's sandy mane stirred in the cool breeze blowing off the moors. 'Saffron seems to want everything just right.'

'Tell me about it!' Alex grumbled, as she mounted the magic pony.

As they rode back down the field to Zoe and Saffron, Alex's mood lightened. Comet was wonderful to ride. She loved the way he moved with a smooth stride, arching his supple neck and holding his head high.

When she stopped next to Zoe and

Maxi, the big brown-and-white pony
turned his head towards Comet and gave
a friendly blow. The two ponies were
already getting on well.

Alex took a deep breath. 'OK. Ready at
last. Who wants to go –' she began.

'Me first!' Saffron was already urging
the grey forward. She and Princess
streaked towards the first fence.

'She's dead keen, isn't she?' Zoe said

47

admiringly, gazing after her cousin.

'That's one way of putting it,' Alex murmured.

They watched as Saffron handled Princess expertly and sailed over all the fences. The grey trotted back to them with her ears pricked.

'Way to go!' Zoe cried. 'That was great!'

'Well done, Saffron!' Alex added. She had to admit that Saffron was a brilliant rider.

Saffron pulled a face. 'Those pathetic jumps are easy-peasy! Princess could almost step over them. We're used to much more challenging ones,' she boasted.

They might be pathetic but they're the best we've got! Alex thought, a bit miffed,

especially after all the fuss Saffron had
made about getting them just right.
Besides, her dad had gone to a lot of
trouble to gather together the poles
and other stuff, so they could have fun
jumping.

Zoe went next. Alex and Saffron sat
side by side, watching and calling out
encouragement from where they sat on
their ponies.

As Maxi cantered towards a fence, Alex
noticed that Zoe was leaning a little too
far forward.

Saffron saw it as well. Her voice
suddenly boomed out. 'For goodness' sake,
sit up straight. And keep your hands and
heels down!'

Zoe almost jumped out of her skin and
jerked on the reins. Maxi slewed sideways

and crashed into the fence, knocking a
pole down.

Alex rode towards her. 'Is Maxi OK?'
she asked worriedly. 'I hope he hasn't hurt
himself.'

Zoe had dismounted and was checking
her pony's knees and legs. 'He seems fine,'
she said.

Saffron looked down from Princess.

'Why didn't you do as I told you?' she demanded.

Alex began helping Zoe to rebuild the fence. 'You'd probably have been all right, if Saffron hadn't yelled at you like that,' she sympathized. 'It put you off your stride.'

Saffron's brows dipped in a fierce frown. 'What's the big deal? I was only trying to help! I can't help it if she didn't listen!'

'Well – maybe if you didn't shout like a foghorn –' Alex began.

'It doesn't matter now,' Zoe cut in hastily. 'I'll do better next time. Your turn, Alex.' She mounted Maxi and then she and Saffron trotted away together to watch.

Alex clicked her tongue at Comet

and he sprang towards the first fence.
He cleared it easily, arching his neck and
proudly tossing his mane. Alex could tell
he was enjoying himself.

Comet soared over all the fences in
turn, until there was just one left. They
were approaching the final fence when
Alex had a sudden flashback to the recent
horse trials where Pasha was injured.

As the chestnut's frightened whinny
seemed to ring in her head, Alex felt her
confidence waver. Maybe she was doing
something wrong when she jumped,
despite what Zoe thought. Could it have
been her fault that Pasha had hurt herself?

She gulped. *What if Comet lands wrong
and hurts himself too . . . ?*

The magic pony slowed down. Alex's
mouth dried as she tried to force down

her fear and work through it. Comet got slower still. He was going to refuse!

'Stop dithering!' Saffron shouted loudly. 'Kick him on. Show him who's boss!'

Alex flushed with annoyance, but managed to get her focus back. She swallowed hard. 'Come on, Comet!' she whispered, pressing him on.

Comet sped up again. He eyed the fence carefully and bounded over it easily.

'Well done!' Alex gasped as they landed safely.

'Are you all right, Alex?' Comet champed at the bit. 'It felt like you didn't really want me to jump. I didn't want to go over it, if you were frightened.'

She leaned down to rub his silky caramel neck. 'I did get scared for a moment when I remembered how Pasha

went lame the last time I was jumping.
I thought I might have done something
wrong that time and I didn't want you to
get hurt too.'

Comet turned his head and blew air
out of his flared nostrils. 'That was not
your fault. Pasha told me on the journey
to your home that she had slipped on a
patch of mud. It was an accident.'

'Really?' Alex said as relief flowed

through her. 'Thanks, Comet. It's great to know that for certain.' She felt a surge of affection for her magic friend as they rode over to Zoe and Saffron.

'That last jump was dead messy,' Saffron criticized. 'To be a good showjumper, you have to keep your mind on what you're doing. Otherwise you won't get anywhere!'

Alex reacted without thinking. 'So I lost concentration for a minute. It's not a crime, is it?' she said sharply.

'I was only saying,' Saffron said huffily. 'Some people are so touchy!'

There was an awkward silence.

Alex saw that Zoe's face had clouded with embarrassment and immediately wished that she'd bitten her tongue. 'Sorry. I didn't mean to snap,' she apologized. 'I guess I'm still a bit worried about Pasha's bad leg.'

Saffron shrugged. 'If you say so. My turn again.' She urged her pony forward. 'Come on, Princess! Let's show them how it's done! Watch and learn, you two amateurs!'

Alex tried to suppress a flicker of irritation. 'Why does she have to be so bossy and full-on all the time? I thought this was supposed to be fun,' she whispered to Comet.

But she must have spoken more loudly that she'd intended, because Zoe heard her.

'Saffron can't help being competitive,' she said, defending her cousin. 'Wouldn't *you* be if your dad expected *you* to follow in his footsteps and be a top showjumper?

Uncle Tim's lovely, but he's really strict.
Give her a chance, Alex. She's OK when
you get to know her better.'

Alex wisely kept silent. She didn't
actually *want* to get to know Saffron
better.

*Why can't it just be me and Comet and
Zoe and Maxi for the school holiday? Like
we'd planned,* she thought wistfully.

'Anyway, we all need to work
extra hard if we're going in for the
showjumping at the Pony Club
fundraising in two weeks' time,' Zoe was
saying.

Alex blinked at her. 'The what?'

'I was going to tell you. Saffron has
entered all three of us. It's a special
surprise.'

Alex was stunned. 'She could have

asked if we even wanted to go in for it!'

Zoe started grinning. 'Duh! Then it
wouldn't have been a surprise, would it,
you muppet?' she teased.

'I guess not.' Alex felt an answering
smile beginning to surface. This was the
first time today that she and Zoe had
laughed together. It felt good – like old
times, when it was just the two of them.

'Clear round – again – for the marvellously talented Saffron Hall-Chapman on the wonderful Sparkly Fairy Princess!' The over-the-top voice echoed around the field as if it was coming out of a loudspeaker at a horse event.

Zoe was giggling as she rode over to her cousin. 'You're a riot, Saffron!'

It was actually pretty funny. Despite herself, Alex managed a smile. She still thought that Zoe's cousin was the bossiest girl she'd ever met, though. How was she going to get on with her for two whole weeks?

But as she stranded Comet's thick mane through her fingers, Alex felt herself calming down. She thought she could probably put up with anything, even Zoe's pushy cousin, as long as she had Comet. He was her own wonderful special secret, never to be shared with anyone.

'I think you deserve a treat, Comet!' Dismounting, she fished in her pocket for a packet of mints and held them up to him on the flat of her hand. She smiled as

the palomino's soft lips nuzzled her hand
as he snuffled them up.

'Delicious!' He crunched them,
spraying bits everywhere and making
Alex laugh.

Chapter
FIVE

Alex fought back tears the following
day. She and her mum stood in the
yard, watching the horse ambulance
disappearing down the winding lane.

The vet had just been to check on
Pasha's leg again. He suspected there
might be complications and the pony was
being taken to a special treatment centre.

'Pasha won't like being away from her

own stable. She's going to miss having her cuddle when I settle her for the night,' Alex gulped.

'Try not to worry about her, love,' Mrs Judd said gently. 'Pasha's in very good hands.'

'I know, but I can't help it. I'm really going to miss her.'

'Course you will. That's natural. So will I.' Her mum gave her a hug. After a while

she said, 'Are you meeting up with Zoe and Saffron today?'

Alex shook her head. 'They're going out for the day with Zoe's aunt and uncle. But we're meeting up here the day after tomorrow so we can do some more jumping. I thought I might go out for a ride up on the moors by myself,' Alex told her.

'Good idea. That'll take your mind off things.'

Mrs Judd stood by as Alex tacked up Comet and then mounted. As she rode out into the yard, her mum reached up and patted the palomino pony's neck.

'Look after her, won't you, boy? She's my special girl.'

Comet whickered softly and pricked his ears.

'I could swear he understands everything you say to him,' her mum said, smiling.

Alex smiled back. 'He does!' *If only her mum knew.*

'See you later!' called Mrs Judd over her shoulder as she went towards the farmhouse.

'Will do!' Alex answered.

As they trotted out of the yard, she spoke to Comet. 'Destiny might be hiding among the rocks and crags. We can search for her.'

His sandy tail flicked up. 'Thank you, Alex.'

At the end of the winding lane, Alex pointed him towards one of the stony tracks that led up to the high moors. Soon they found themselves in a stark landscape, under huge open skies.

Alex loved it up here. Drystone walls snaked across the hillside, where sheep and their lambs grazed on the scrubby grass. Here and there enormous jagged grey stones thrust upwards from the bare soil like sleeping giants of old. Some of them were grouped together, forming natural shelters and hiding places.

'Hold tight!' Comet shot forward like a rocket and Alex felt a glow of excitement.

Tiny rainbows glimmered in his mane as his shining hooves ate up the ground. She felt a warm tingling feeling flow to the end of her fingertips and his magic swirled round her, keeping her safe as they galloped as fast as the wind. She knew that she'd never get tired of riding the magic pony.

'Yay! Go, Comet, go!' she shouted, her voice ringing out across the expanse of moorland.

Comet raked the landscape with his keen eyes, looking for any signs of his lost twin. Alex kept her eyes peeled too. They explored the rock formations and hidden spaces. But all they saw were three walkers climbing a stile and a farmer on a tractor checking his flock.

There was no sign of any ponies.

The ground sloped gradually upwards and the soil became thin and stony. Pink and purple heather clothed the ground and grew in cracks in the stones. Comet galloped on tirelessly, but they found no trace of Destiny.

Alex suggested that they search lower down among the winding lanes and farm buildings. The sun came out, turning Comet's caramel coat and sandy mane and tail to molten gold. Cloud shadows rippled across the sloping moors.

Suddenly, Comet stiffened. Catching a movement from the corner of his eye, he laid back his ears.

'What's wrong?' she asked him.

'A dark horse is close!' he neighed in panic.

Alex couldn't see anything but, before she could catch her breath, Comet bolted straight for a gap in a broken wooden fence. He was going to barge through it!

Alex caught sight of the dull sheen of metal. There was barbed wire strung across the gap, but Comet hadn't noticed it.

'Stop!' she cried, pulling on the reins.

But Comet pounded on, blinded by his terror of the enemy horses from his world, who wanted to steal his power. The dangerous fence was right in front of them!

One step. Two steps. Three . . .

In desperation Alex sawed at the reins. 'Stop, Comet!' she begged. 'There's nothing there!'

It did the trick. Comet came to his

senses. But he stopped so suddenly that
Alex lost her balance. She flew forward,
right over his head and crashed into the
fence.

The fence's rotten wood collapsed
beneath her, breaking her fall. 'Oh!' she
gasped as the barbed wire tore into her
jeans and pain shot through her leg.

Biting her lip, she tore herself free and
stumbled to her feet. She limped towards
Comet, desperate to make sure he was all
right.

The magic pony's sides were heaving and he sucked air noisily through his flared nostrils.

'It's OK. You're safe,' Alex soothed gently. 'It was only a trick of the light as the shadows moved across the hills.'

Gradually, Comet grew calm.

'You risked yourself to save me. Thank you, Alex,' he whickered fondly, lowering his head to gently nudge her arm.

'Anyone would have done the same,' she said, cupping his velvety nose.

'No, they would not. You are a very special friend, Alex.'

A soft cloud of his warm hay-scented breath enveloped her and Alex's heart swelled with love for her magic pony. She reached up and put her arms round Comet's neck. Closing her eyes, she

pressed her cheek to his silky warmth.
After a few moments of wonderful
closeness that she would never forget, she
drew back.

'Mum will have lunch ready. We'd
better go . . . oh!' She winced. Now that
the excitement was over, her injured leg
began to throb horribly.

Comet's eyes widened with concern.
'You are hurt! I will help you!'

Alex felt another tingling sensation
flowing down to her fingertips as violet
sparks bloomed in Comet's caramel coat
and a glittering mist filled with hundreds
of tiny stars rose into the air. It floated
down and surrounded her leg, where it
swirled briefly before sinking into her
torn jeans and disappearing.

The sharp pain seemed to melt away

like the morning mist on the moors. As Alex watched, the edges of her ripped jeans drew together and mended themselves.

'Thanks, Comet! I feel much better now.'

Comet swivelled his ears. 'You are welcome. Climb back on my back, Alex. Let us return.'

Alex did so. Thorn bushes and drystone walls sped past and soon they were approaching the winding lane that led to Scarp Hill Farm. Comet gave an excited neigh as he slowed to a halt. Stretching out his neck, he looked at the ground.

Alex peered over his shoulder to see what he was looking at.

She did a double take.

Stretching ahead of them and curving

away out of sight behind a nearby
farmyard was a faint line of softly glowing
violet hoof-prints.

'What's that?' Alex asked in wonder.

'It's Destiny's trail! She has been here!'
Comet told her.

Alex gasped. Did that mean that the

magic pony was leaving – right now – to go after his twin? 'Is . . . is she somewhere close?' she asked him anxiously.

'No. This trail is cold. But at least I know that Destiny came this way. When I am closer to her I will sense her presence and I will also hear her hoof-beats.'

'Will I be able to hear them too?' she asked, starting to relax a bit.

'Yes, if you are riding me or we are close together. But other humans will not be able to hear them.' His glowing eyes grew serious. 'I may have to leave suddenly, without saying goodbye, to catch up with Destiny.'

Alex fought against a new feeling of dismay. She didn't think she would ever be ready to lose her friend. 'Once . . . once you find her, you could both stay

here with me, couldn't you?' she asked
hopefully in a wobbly voice.

Comet shook his head. 'I am afraid that
is not possible. We must return to our
family on Rainbow Mist Island. I hope
you understand, Alex?'

Alex nodded sadly. She swallowed hard
as she tried not to think about Comet
leaving and promised herself that she was
going to enjoy every single moment spent
with him.

Chapter
SIX

'Ta-dah! How about that for a water jump?' Alex said with a proud flourish.

She was in the lower field with Zoe and Saffron and their ponies. There was a large muddy puddle at the bottom of a slope. Earlier, her dad had helped her to position a row of logs along its shortest side.

'Perfect!' Zoe said, smiling.

Saffron shrugged, unimpressed. 'It's not bad, I suppose.' Her matching hat cover, gloves and designer gilet were the colour of lime milkshake today and she held a dainty little riding whip.

Alex felt conscious of her muddy boots, old jeans and battered body warmer. She was glad that Zoe was dressed in similar practical clothes.

They all lined up at the water jump.

Zoe and Maxi went first. The brown–

and–white pony landed well, picking up his feet as he cantered on to dry grass. Alex went next: Comet jumped perfectly, leaping over the logs and splashing through the water. He even bucked playfully when he'd finished.

Alex laughed aloud. To herself she murmured, 'Find fault with that, if you can, Saffron.'

Princess, on the other hand, obviously didn't fancy getting wet. As Saffron rode her towards the logs, the grey pony shied. Taken by surprise, Saffron almost lost her balance. She only just managed to keep her seat as Princess stuck her nose in the air and pranced cheekily round the puddle.

Zoe and Alex laughed at the pony's antics.

Saffron flushed bright red. 'Come on, Princess. Stop being naughty!' Pressing her lips together, she lined her pony up again.

Princess champed at the bit, threw up her head and slowed right down, about to refuse again. Saffron gave her a light tap on the rump with the whip. The grey pony sprang over the log from a standing position and stopped dead in the middle of the puddle.

Alex was helpless with laughter. Princess was really playing up today.

Comet whickered, rolling back his lips as if he was laughing too.

But Saffron had a face like thunder. 'What's wrong with you?' she grumbled to her pony. 'You're making me look really stupid!'

'Why don't you just try talking to her
gently while you squeeze her on?' Alex
suggested reasonably.

'I know what I'm doing! Dad's shown
me how to deal with a stubborn pony!'
Saffron retorted. She hit her pony on the
rump, but Princess still refused to move.

'I'd like to see how Saffron would like

it if someone hit her!' Alex whispered crossly to Comet. 'Maybe someone should grab that whip!'

The magic pony's deep violet eyes glowed with purpose.

Alex felt a familiar tingling sensation flow down to her fingertips as Comet opened his mouth and huffed out a large breath, which turned into a tiny violet fireball. It shot invisibly towards Saffron and Princess trailing tiny bright stars. The fireball burst above them, showering them with violet glitter before dissolving harmlessly. Saffron gasped with surprise as the dainty riding whip flew out of her hand, whizzed through the air and landed two metres away.

At the same time, Princess lowered her head and began pawing at the water.

Saffron was still looking at where the
whip had landed and didn't seem to have
noticed, but Zoe read the telltale signs.

'Oh no! Princess is going to roll! Watch
out, Saffron!' she warned her cousin.

It was too late. The grey pony sank to
her knees as she lowered herself into the
puddle.

'Oo-er!' Saffron lost her balance.
She slipped forward, did an impressive
somersault and landed on her bottom.
As Princess rolled over, a wave of muddy
water sloshed all over Saffron, soaking her
from head to foot.

Princess stood up, shook herself and
calmly trotted to dry land.

Alex clapped her hands over her
mouth. 'Oh dear,' she said in a muffled
voice, trying without success to stem the

laughter that was bubbling up inside her. 'I didn't expect that to happen.'

Her magical friend blinked at her with surprised long-lashed eyes. 'I thought that was what you wanted.'

Zoe dismounted and ran to help her cousin. 'Are you OK?'

'Does it look like it?' Saffron burst into tears. 'My clothes are ruined! They were a birthday present.' Dripping, she lumbered

through the mud and squelched up the field.

Seeing that Saffron was really upset, Alex abruptly stopped laughing. She felt an uncomfortable stirring of guilt.

Comet had only used his magic because she had grumbled to him about Saffron. Alex chewed at her lip, wondering what she could do to set things right. Saffron had caught up with Princess. She grasped her bridle in a muddy hand. 'Dad's going to go ballistic if I take her back looking like this. She's filthy!' she wailed.

'Don't worry. I'll tell Uncle Tim it was an accident,' Zoe said.

'It won't make any difference. He'll still blame me. You know how strict he can be. He's got this saying. "It's always the rider's fault."'

'But that's not fair!' Alex exclaimed.

Unexpectedly, she felt herself starting to feel sorry for the older girl. It couldn't be much fun having a dad who was so strict. She thought hard and a plan began to form in her mind.

'Hang on! I know what to do. Let's go to my house . . .'

Chapter
SEVEN

'Oh my goodness!' Mrs Judd exclaimed
when she saw Saffron standing miserably
in the utility room, dripping mud and
water everywhere.

To Alex's relief, her mum didn't waste
time asking for explanations.

Mrs Judd rolled up her sleeves. 'Right.
Let's get you out of those wet clothes and
into a shower. Alex can you fetch me –'

'Sorry, Mum. I've got something mega-important to do,' Alex interrupted swiftly. 'Zoe will help; won't you, Zoe?'

'Um . . . sure.' Zoe frowned, puzzled.

'Towels are in the bathroom. And help yourself to any dry clothes from my bedroom,' Alex called over her shoulder, dashing outside before anyone could protest.

She zoomed over to the stables, where all three ponies were tethered. Comet whinnied a greeting when he saw her.

Alex looked at Princess in dismay.

The once elegant grey pony was
covered with patches of smelly drying
mud and streaked with grass stains. Her
tangled mane and tail looked like frayed
rope.

'Wow! She's in an awful mess, isn't she?'
Alex found herself wondering whether
there would be time to put her plan into
action. But she had to try.

First though, she had an admission to
make to her magical friend.

'I'm . . . I'm sorry that I encouraged
you to use your magic when I was cross.
It was wrong of me, Comet. I know that
now. Can you forgive me?'

'Of course. Everyone makes mistakes,'
the magic pony said generously. 'But
it is what you do to put them right

that is important.'

Alex felt a bit better. 'Thanks, Comet. You're the best. I've got an idea. This is how I can make it up with Saffron . . .'

The magic pony swivelled his ears, listening carefully as Alex told him what she had in mind. '. . . but we'll have to hurry before Zoe, Saffron or my mum come out here.'

Comet nodded. 'I will help you. But are you certain that this is what you want?' he asked, his eyes sparkling mischievously.

Alex didn't hesitate. 'This time – definitely!'

She felt a familiar warm tingling sensation flowing down to the tips of her fingers. Large violet sparks ignited in Comet's caramel-coloured coat and a cloud of tiny bright lights like busy worker bees fluttered into the air. The glittering little helpers spread out, gathering everything they needed before they got to work. Alex watched in astonishment.

Splash! A hose sprayed warm soapy water over Princess, washing the mud from her coat, mane and tail. *Swish!*

Towels swept back and forth drying her.
Rustle! Brushes buffed her coat, and
combs gently untangled her mane and
tail.

Princess sighed with contentment,
enjoying being pampered. She even lifted
each hoof in turn for it to be picked
out, brushed and oiled. Finally she was
finished. Her coat gleamed like silver and
her mane and tail were brushed to glossy
silkiness.

'She looks wonderful. Thanks, Comet!'

'I am glad that I could help,' Comet
neighed, as every last little glowing bee
disappeared and the deep violet sparks
faded from his coat.

They were only just in time. Zoe
and Saffron were leaving the house and
crossing the yard.

Saffron's eye widened when she saw
Princess. 'Alex? What . . . Wow! I can't
believe it!' she gasped delightedly. She was
dressed in one of Alex's jumpers and a
spare pair of jodhpurs, which were tucked
into a pair of her mum's old riding boots.

'How did you manage to get Princess
looking like that?' Zoe asked.

*You wouldn't believe me, even if I could
tell you!* she thought. 'I love a challenge!
Anyway, I didn't want to hang around,
getting bored, while everyone fussed over
Saffron,' she fibbed happily.

While Saffron was admiring her
perfectly groomed pony, Zoe leaned close
to whisper to Alex. 'You can't fool me.
You did it to stop Saffron getting into
trouble, didn't you?'

Alex shrugged. 'Well, I did feel a bit

sorry for her. I didn't want her to get into hot water with her dad.' She would have loved to tell Zoe the truth, but she couldn't do that without giving away Comet's secret. She knew that she would never tell anyone about her magical friend.

Comet seemed to know what she was thinking. He tossed his head and gave a soft whicker of approval.

Saffron turned to Alex. 'Thanks, Alex. I won't forget this,' she said warmly. 'I . . . I know I can be a pain. It's the way I am, but I don't mean anything by it. Friends, OK?'

Alex flushed. 'I guess I haven't been that easy to get on with either,' she admitted honestly. 'It'll be different from now on.'

'Yay!' Zoe did a little dance of triumph. 'Does this mean we can all concentrate on having fun and getting ready for the Pony Club fundraising? I've got a space on my mirror that's rosette shaped!'

'You bet!' Alex and Saffron chorused happily.

Chapter
EIGHT

Comet's warm magic swirled round Alex
as they paused on the heathery hillside a
week later. His sides were heaving after
a thrilling gallop and as he looked out
across the wide expanse of the fells he
caught his breath.

Alex relaxed in the saddle, full of the
afterglow of another exciting ride on the
magic pony. If she lived to be a hundred,

she would never forget the joy of riding
him.

She had spent the afternoon at Zoe's
house, watching some of Saffron's
showjumping DVDs. Zoe's mum had got
in some nibbles and dips and pizza slices,
and turned the event into a party.

Now Alex and Comet were cutting
across the moors on their way home.

Another search among the rock
formations had proved fruitless. There had
been no more signs of Destiny.

'It was so much fun today and Saffron
was great. We're all getting along better.
But Zoe will always be my best friend,'
Alex told him happily, resting her hands
in her lap.

Comet huffed out a warm breath and
snorted softly. 'I am glad that things have
worked out well for you.'

Alex thought she detected a trace of
sadness in his voice and guessed that he
was missing his twin sister.

'They'll work out for you and Destiny
too,' she said kindly. 'I know they will.'

Comet's eyes glowed with new hope.
'I hope so. Thank you, Alex.'

Grey clouds were gathering above the

huge boulders. Alex shivered and reached out to stroke the palomino's silky neck. 'It's getting cold. There's a warm stable and a bucket of oats waiting for you at home. Shall we go?'

Comet pricked his ears. 'I am ready. Hold tight!'

Alex caught her breath as the magic pony rocked back on to his hind legs and pawed the air with his hooves. As he leapt forward, tiny rainbows glimmered in his caramel coat and sandy mane.

They galloped towards a stony track and in no time at all reached the winding lane that led to Scarp Hill Farm. Comet smoothly changed pace and Alex rose to the trot as the farmhouse came into view.

Her heart gave a lurch as she spotted

a lorry in the yard. It was the horse
ambulance. 'Pasha's back from the
specialist centre!' she cried delightedly.

Dismounting quickly, she led Comet
into the stable.

'Pasha!' The chestnut pony was in her
stall. At the sound of Alex's voice, she
pricked her ears. Turning her head, she
nickered and gave a friendly blow. Comet
snorted softly to her and the ponies
gently touched noses.

'Oh, that's so sweet. Pasha looks loads
happier, doesn't she?' Alex stroked her
pony's nose.

She quickly unsaddled the magic pony
and gave him a scoop of food to munch,
before rushing into the house to talk to
her mum.

Simon Green, the vet, was sitting at the

table, drinking a mug of tea. He looked up and smiled. 'Hi, Alex.'

'Hi, Simon. Hi, Mum. I've just seen Pasha! She looks great! Has the treatment worked? When can I exercise her on a lunge rope in the yard? How soon can I ride her again?' Eager questions spilled out of her.

'Slow down, love!' Mrs Judd cautioned. 'I think you should listen to what Simon has to say before you get your hopes up. Isn't that right, Simon?'

The vet nodded. 'The treatment she had was something very new, involving stem cells. It seemed to go well, but I'm afraid we can't expect miracles . . .'

Alex felt her high spirits sinking as she listened to Simon explaining that it could be weeks before they knew whether the treatment had worked. 'Does . . . does that mean Pasha's leg might never get better?'

'I think there's a fair chance that it will. But it's best to be prepared just in case,' came the vet's reply. 'As I say, miracles are rare.'

A fair chance? What did that mean? It didn't sound all that hopeful. Alex felt her high spirits sinking to rock bottom.

After Simon left, Alex went back out to the stable. She found Comet standing with his head very close to Pasha's. The little chestnut pony's eyes were closed and she had a blissful look on her face.

As Comet sensed Alex's presence, he looked up and stepped back from Pasha. His eyes glowed like amethysts. It was a look that sank deep inside her chest and made her heart flutter.

'Comet –' Alex began.

But before she could finish her question, Alex heard the sound that she had been hoping for and dreading at the same time: the hollow sound of galloping hooves overhead.

She froze. Destiny was here! There was no mistake.

Comet raced past her out of the stable.

Alex ran after him to a corner of the yard where a twinkling rainbow mist was drifting down. In the middle of it Comet

stood in his true form, a palomino pony
no longer. Rainbow droplets gleamed on
his noble arched neck, cream coat and
flowing golden mane and tail; magnificent
gold-feathered wings sprang from his
powerful shoulders.

'Comet!' Alex gasped. She had almost
forgotten how beautiful he was. 'You . . .
you're leaving right now, aren't you?'

His wonderful violet eyes lost a little
of their brightness for a second. 'I must.
If I am to catch Destiny and save her
from our enemies.'

Alex's throat burned with tears; she
knew she must find the courage to
let her friend go. She hurried towards
him. Leaning against Comet's glowing
shoulder, she rested her face against his
warm silken cheek.

'I'll never forget you,' she murmured adoringly.

'I will not forget you either, Alex. You have been a good friend,' Comet neighed softly. He allowed her to hug him one last time and then gently backed away. 'Farewell. Ride well and true,' he said in a deep musical voice.

There was a final flash of violet light and a silent explosion of rainbow sparkles that floated down around Alex and tinkled like miniature bells as they hit the ground.

Comet spread his golden wings and soared upwards. He faded and was gone.

Alex wiped away tears, hardly able to believe that everything had happened so quickly. Something lay in the yard. It was a single glittering gold wing feather.

Bending down, she picked it up.

The feather tingled against her fingers
as it faded to a cream colour. Alex slipped
it into her pocket. She would always keep
the feather to remind herself of the magic

106

pony and the wonderful adventure they had shared.

As she turned back towards the stable, she heard a soft neigh. Her little chestnut pony came out and cantered round the yard in a perfect circle, before walking towards her. *Look at me, I'm all well again*, she seemed to be saying.

'Pasha! You're not lame any more!' Alex gasped delightedly. A smile broke out on her face as she knew that this was Comet's final gift to her. 'You were wrong, Simon. Miracles can happen . . . when you have a magic pony's help!'

Pasha nudged her arm gently and blew sweet breath on to her neck. Alex threw her arms round her pony's neck and breathed out a long sigh of perfect happiness.

'Thank you so much, Comet. Take care.
And I hope you and Destiny get back
safely to Rainbow Mist Island.'

Out Now

Magic Ponies

Could you be a little pony's special friend?

Magic Ponies

A New Friend

SUE BENTLEY

puffin.co.uk

Out Now

Magic Ponies

Could you be a little pony's special friend?

Magic Ponies

A Special Wish

SUE BENTLEY

puffin.co.uk

Out Now

Magic Ponies

Could you be a little pony's special friend?

Magic Ponies

A Twinkle of Hooves

SUE BENTLEY

puffin.co.uk

Coming Soon

puffin.co.uk

OUT NOW

A **purrfect** recipe for fun!

puffin.co.uk

Magic Ponies

A New Friend

A Special Wish

A Twinkle of Hooves

Showjumping Dreams

Seaside Summer

Riding Rescue

Magic Puppy

A New Beginning
9780141323503

Muddy Paws
9780141323510

Cloud Capers
9780141323527

Star of the Show
9780141323534

Party Dreams
9780141323794

A Forest Charm
9780141323800

Twirling Tails
9780141323817

School of Mischief
9780141323824

Snowy Wishes
9780141323831

Classroom Princess
9780141324791

Friendship Forever
9780141324784

Sparkling Skates
9780141324777

Sunshine Shimmers
9780141324760

Spellbound at School
9780141324753

Coming Soon

The Perfect Secret
9780141324746

A little puppy
a sprinkling of magic,
a forever friend

If you like
Magic Puppy,
you'll love

Magic Kitten

A Summer Spell
9780141320144

Classroom Chaos
9780141320151

Star Dreams
9780141320168

Double Trouble
9780141320175

Moonlight Mischief
9780141321530

A Circus Wish
9780141321547

Sparkling Steps
9780141321554

A Glittering Gallop
9780141321561

Seaside Mystery
9780141321981

Firelight Friends
9780141321998

A Shimmering Splash
9780141322001

A Puzzle of Paws
9780141322018

A Christmas Surprise
9780141323237

Picture Perfect
9780141323480

A Splash of Forever
9780141323497

More

Magic Kitten

Fun!

Magical Activity Book
978–0–141–32294–0

Sparkling Sticker Book
978–0–141–32293–3

Enter a world of purrfect Magic Kitten fun
with fabulous things to make, do and draw
– and over 100 sparkling stickers!

It all started with a Scarecrow

Puffin is well over sixty years old.
Sounds ancient, doesn't it? But Puffin has never been
so lively. We're always on the lookout for the next big
idea, which is how it began all those years ago.

Penguin Books was a big idea from the mind of
a man called Allen Lane, who in 1935 invented
the quality paperback and changed the world.
**And from great Penguins, great Puffins grew,
changing the face of children's books forever.**

The first four Puffin Picture Books were hatched in 1940 and the
first Puffin story book featured a man with broomstick arms called
Worzel Gummidge. In 1967 Kaye Webb, Puffin Editor, started the
Puffin Club, promising to **'make children into readers'**.
She kept that promise and over 200,000 children became
devoted Puffineers through their quarterly installments of
Puffin Post, which is now back for a new generation.

Many years from now, we hope you'll look back and
remember Puffin with a smile. **No matter what your age
or what you're into, there's a Puffin for everyone.**
The possibilities are endless, but one thing is for sure:
whether it's a picture book or a paperback, a sticker book
or a hardback, **if it's got that little Puffin
on it – it's bound to be good.**